W9-BRY-510

PACK 109

by Mike Thaler

pictures by Normand Chartier

SCHOLASTIC INC.
New York Toronto London Auckland Sydney

for Rose Eisenstein
our fairy godmother-in-law

M.T.

This one's especially
for Samuel Gerard.

N.C.

 Published by Scholastic Inc., 555 Broadway,
New York, NY 10012, by arrangement with Puffin Books,
a division of Penguin Books USA Inc.
Printed in the U.S.A.
ISBN 0-590-48751-5

18171615141312 23 02 01 00

Contents

The Kite 8

Making Cookies 18

Knots 28

Morse Code 36

First Aid 42

Pack 109 meets in the woods.

Pack 109 has five forest scouts.

Every time they meet,

they do their best to get

another merit badge.

The Kite

"Today we are going

to make a kite," said Tooth.

"Okay," said Chip,

who always agreed with him.

"We need two sticks," said Nutsy.

"And some cloth," said Rat.

"And some string," said Eek.

So they went and got two sticks, some cloth, and some string.

Tooth tied the two sticks together.

"Good," said Chip.

Then Rat covered them with cloth.

Eek tied on the string.

"It's a kite!" said Chip.

"Not until it flies," said Nutsy.

"I'll fly it," said Tooth.

So Tooth grabbed the string and started to run across the field.

The kite bumped on the ground behind him.

He ran back.

The kite bumped some more.

"You need a tail," said Rat.

"I have a tail," said Tooth.

"On the *kite,*" said Nutsy.

So they made a tail and tied it on the kite.

Tooth grabbed the string again.

He ran across the field.

The kite bounced behind him.

He ran back.

The kite bounced some more.

"You need a longer tail,"

said Rat.

"My tail is plenty long,"

said Tooth,

throwing down the string.

"Wait," said Eek,

"I think what we need is wind."

So they all sat down in the shade

and waited.

Finally the wind began to blow.
It lifted the kite into the sky
and carried it away.
"We did it!" shouted Tooth.

And they ran and sewed on their

KITE FLYING MERIT BADGES.

Making Cookies

"Today we are going
to make cookies," said Tooth.
"What kind of cookies?"
asked Eek.
"Chocolate chip cookies."

"We need flour, sugar, eggs,
and chocolate chips," said Tooth.
They all went off.
Soon they came back with flour,
sugar, and eggs.

“We couldn’t find any chips,”

said Nutsy.

“But we need *chips,*”

said Tooth.

Everyone looked at Chip.

"Not me!" said Chip.

"Well, we'll just have to make
cookies without chips,"
said Nutsy.

"Thank you," said Chip.

So they mixed the flour,

sugar, and eggs together.

They made little round cookies

and left them in the sun to bake.

Two hours later

the cookies were ready.

"I'll try one first," said Tooth.

He picked up a cookie.

"Heavy," he said.

He put the cookie in his mouth
and bit down.
"Ouch!" said Tooth,
grabbing his tooth.
"Are they hard?" said Chip.
Tooth nodded his head.

"Very hard?" asked Rat.

Tooth nodded again.

"As hard as *rocks*?"

said Eek.

"Yes," nodded Tooth.

"Great!" said Eek.

He gathered

all the cookies together.

"What are you doing?"

asked Nutsy.

"Rock collecting," smiled Eek.

Everyone nodded.

Then they all sewed on their

ROCK COLLECTING MERIT BADGES.

Knots

“Today we are going

to tie knots,” said Tooth.

“Good idea,” said Chip.

“Here is some rope,” said Rat.

“I’ll show you how,”

said Tooth, taking the rope.

He squiggled it all up into a ball.

"There," he said, "that is a knot."

"That's not a knot,"

said Nutsy.

He took the rope.

It hung straight down.

“Here,” said Rat, “I’ll show you.”

He rumpled the rope up

into a ball.

“That’s not a knot either,”

said Nutsy.

He held up the rope.

It dangled straight down.

“What is a knot?” asked Eek.

“I do not know what is a knot,”

said Nutsy. “But I do know

what is not.”

"Is a knot a wrinkle?" asked Eek.

"Sort of," said Nutsy.

"Is a knot a twist?" asked Eek.

"Kind of," said Nutsy.

"I give up," said Eek.

He started to walk away.

"Hey," said Chip,

"your shoe is untied."

"Oh," said Eek.

He sat down and tied it.

"Wait!" shouted Nutsy.

"That's a knot! That's a knot!"

Everyone stared at Eek's shoelace.

"That's a knot," they all agreed.

So they sewed on their

KNOT TYING MERIT BADGES.

Morse Code

“Today we are going to send

messages in Morse code,”

said Tooth.

He held up a flashlight.

He flashed it twice.

"What did I say?" he asked.

"Blow your nose," said Chip.

"That's not what I said," Tooth said.

"Walk the dog," said Rat.

"Not even close," said Tooth.

"Walk your nose," said Nutsy.

“I’ll try something else,”

said Tooth.

He flashed it three times.

“Wash the car,” said Chip.

“Blow your nose,” said Rat.

“Wash your nose,” said Nutsy.

“You guys are terrible,”

said Tooth.

"I'll try once more."

He flashed it four times.

"There's a wart on your nose,"

said Chip.

"Take off your hat," said Rat.

"Take off your nose," said Nutsy.

Tooth threw down the flashlight.

"I know what that means," said Eek.

"What?" said Tooth.

"YOU GIVE UP!" said Eek.

"That's right," said Tooth.

They looked at each other.

They nodded.

They knew what *that* meant.

So they all went and sewed on their

MORSE CODE MERIT BADGES.

First Aid

"Today we are going to learn first aid,"

said Tooth.

He held up a roll of gauze.

"Great," said Nutsy,

"we'll wrap you up."

"Why not wrap Rat?" said Tooth.

"He's too small," said Nutsy.

"Okay," said Tooth, "you can wrap me.

But be careful."

They wrapped Tooth's right leg.

They wrapped Tooth's left leg.

They wrapped his body.

They wrapped his arms.

“I don’t like this,” said Tooth.

He started to walk away.

He fell over

and hit his head on a log.

"We better wrap his head, too,"

said Nutsy.

They wrapped up Tooth's head.

"Now let's sew on our

FIRST AID MERIT BADGES,"

said Chip.

So they did.

Then they sewed one on Tooth, too.